This Book Belongs To:

The Oakwood Monster

"The ground grew dark and the monster grabbed the little mouse…" Billy Jo Bunny whispered to Fluffy and Sherry Squirrel. They should have been sleeping, but instead they were telling each other scary stories.

"Last night I saw a dark shadow," Sherry whispered, "A big, black, shadow."

Fluffy's eyes grew large. "Really?" she asked.

Sherry nodded. "Must have been a monster."

The next day, Sherry was painting pictures with Benson at the bear's tree house. Lily, Benson's pet bug, felt left out and pouted at the edge of the table. Suddenly, Lily sprang to her feet and ran through the paint and across both of their pictures.

"Lily!" Sherry complained, "You've ruined my picture!"

"Lily, that wasn't very nice," Benson said.

While Benson was looking at the footprints across his picture, something dark appeared in the window. Across the room, Sherry watched the shadow grow. "It's a monster!" she cried.

"What monster?" Benson asked. Then he looked at the window; there was nothing there.

"It was there!" Sherry exclaimed.

Benson thought for a moment. "Maybe it was Christopher, but he's just a little crow," said Benson.

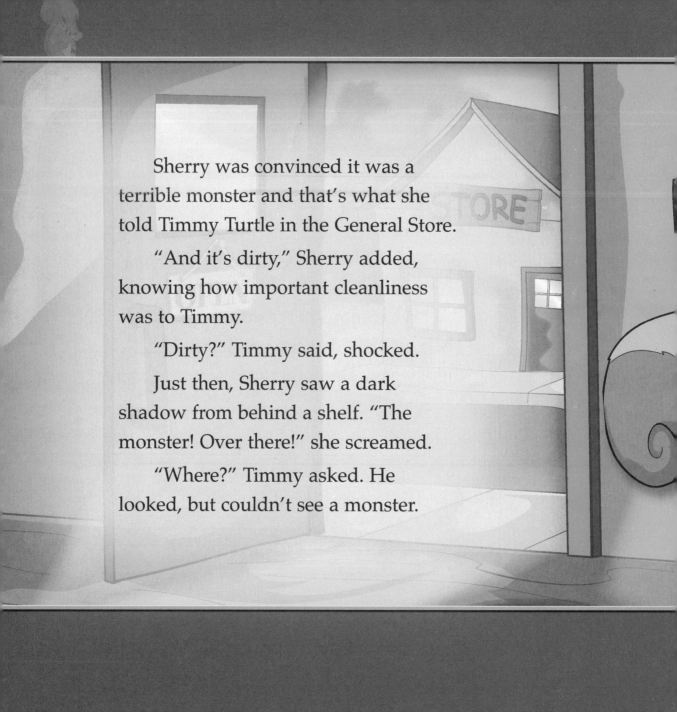

Sherry was convinced it was a terrible monster and that's what she told Timmy Turtle in the General Store.

"And it's dirty," Sherry added, knowing how important cleanliness was to Timmy.

"Dirty?" Timmy said, shocked.

Just then, Sherry saw a dark shadow from behind a shelf. "The monster! Over there!" she screamed.

"Where?" Timmy asked. He looked, but couldn't see a monster.

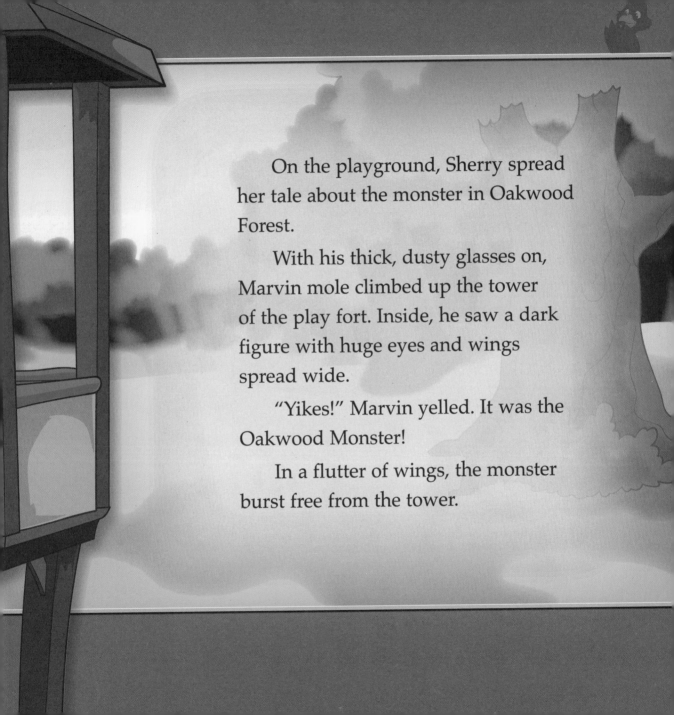

On the playground, Sherry spread her tale about the monster in Oakwood Forest.

With his thick, dusty glasses on, Marvin mole climbed up the tower of the play fort. Inside, he saw a dark figure with huge eyes and wings spread wide.

"Yikes!" Marvin yelled. It was the Oakwood Monster!

In a flutter of wings, the monster burst free from the tower.

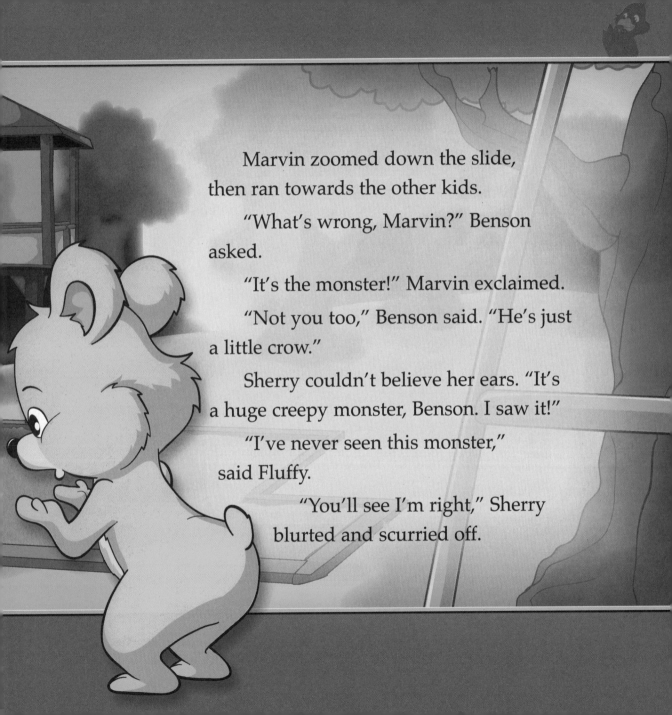

Marvin zoomed down the slide, then ran towards the other kids.

"What's wrong, Marvin?" Benson asked.

"It's the monster!" Marvin exclaimed.

"Not you too," Benson said. "He's just a little crow."

Sherry couldn't believe her ears. "It's a huge creepy monster, Benson. I saw it!"

"I've never seen this monster," said Fluffy.

"You'll see I'm right," Sherry blurted and scurried off.

On Sunday, everyone gathered for a picnic. Rosey Robin and Old Blue found young Christopher Crow, alone and sad.

"How about you go on and play with the others over there," Old Blue said.

"They don't like me," the little crow said. Big tears filled his eyes and dropped down his cheeks.

"They just don't know you," Rosey said. "Not yet."

Old Blue carried the little crow over to the other kids. "This here's Christopher," he said.

With a frightened flap of his wings, timid little Christopher suddenly flew up. His dark shadow grew large on the ground.

"The monster!" Sherry screamed.

The rest of the kids looked up to see only Christopher. "That's the Oakwood Monster?" they laughed.

"Sherry, how about you partner up with Christopher for your game?" Old Blue asked.

"Okay," Sherry reluctantly agreed.

The relay game began. Sherry ran with an acorn; then Christopher flew and dropped it in the basket. Christopher could fly faster than any of them could run, so even though Sherry had the shortest legs of anybody, they finished long before the others.